THE UNOFFICIAL SPY

BY

ARTHUR B. REEVE

British Library Cataloguing-in-Publication Data
A catalogue record for this book is available from the
British Library

Arthur Benjamin Reeve

Arthur Benjamin Reeve was born on 15th October 1880 in New York, USA.

Reeve received his University education at Princeton and upon graduating enrolled at the New York Law School. However, his career was not destined to be in the field of Law. Between 1910 and 1918 he produced 82 short stories for Cosmopolitan magazine featuring his super-sleuth Professor Craig Kennedy. Kennedy is sometimes referred to as "The American Sherlock Holmes" due to his astounding ability at crime solving and his Watson-like sidekick Walter Jameson, a newspaper reporter. These characters featured in 18 novels, some of which were pseudo-novels stitched together from various short stories.

During this period he also began authoring screenplays, beginning with *The Exploits of Elaine* (1914). By the end of this decade his film career was at its peak with his name appearing on seven films, most of them serials and three of them starring Harry Houdini. Due to the film industry's migration to the west coast of America and Reeve's desire to remain in the east he produced less and less work for film. However, in 1927 he entered into a contract to write film scenarios for notorious millionaire-murderer, Harry K. Thaw, on the subject of fake spiritualists. The deal resulted in a lawsuit when Thaw refused to pay. In late 1928, Reeve declared bankruptcy.

Reeve continued to write detective stories for pulp magazines, but also covered many celebrated crime cases for various newspapers, including the murder of William Desmond Taylor, and the trial of Lindbergh baby kidnapper, Bruno Hauptmann. During the 1930s he became an anti-rackets crusader and produced a work of history on the subject titled *The Golden Age of Crime* (1931).

In 1932 he moved to Trenton to be near his alma mater. He died on 9th August 1936.

THE UNOFFICIAL SPY

"Craig, do you see that fellow over by the desk, talking to the night clerk?" I asked Kennedy as we lounged into the lobby of the new Hotel Vanderveer one evening after reclaiming our hats from the plutocrat who had acquired the checking privilege. We had dined on the roof garden of the Vanderveer apropos of nothing at all except our desire to become acquainted with a new hotel.

"Yes," replied Kennedy, "what of him?"

"He's the house detective, McBride. Would you like to meet him? He's full of good stories, an interesting chap. I met him at a dinner given to the President not long ago and he told me a great yarn about how the secret service, the police, and the hotel combined to guard the President during the dinner. You know, a big hotel is the stamping ground for all sorts of cranks and crooks."

The house detective had turned and had caught my eye. Much to my surprise, he advanced to meet me.

"Say, - er - er - Jameson," he began, at last recalling my name, though he had seen me only once and then for only a short time. "You're on the Star, I believe?"

"Yes," I replied, wondering what he could want.

"Well - er - do you suppose you could do the house a little - er - favour?" he asked, hesitating and dropping his voice.

"What is it?" I queried, not feeling certain but that it was a veiled attempt to secure a little free advertising for the Vanderveer. "By the way, let me introduce you to my friend Kennedy, McBride."

"Craig Kennedy?" he whispered aside, turning quickly to me. I nodded.

"Mr. Kennedy," exclaimed the house man deferentially, "are you very busy just now?"

"Not especially so," replied Craig. "My friend Jameson was telling me that you knew some interesting yarns about hotel detective life. I should like to hear you tell some of them, if you are not yourself too - "

"Perhaps you'd rather see one instead?" interrupted the house detective, eagerly scanning Craig's face.

"Indeed, nothing could please me more. What is it - a 'con' man or a hotel 'beat'?"

McBride looked about to make sure that no one was listening. "Neither," he whispered. "It's either a suicide or a murder. Come upstairs with me. There isn't a man in the world I would rather have met at this very instant, Mr. Kennedy, than yourself."

We followed McBride into an elevator which he stopped at the fifteenth floor. With a nod to the young woman who was the floor clerk, the house detective led the way down the thickly carpeted hall, stopping at a room which, we could see through the transom, was lighted. He drew a bunch of keys from his pocket and inserted a pass key into the lock.

The door swung open into a sumptuously fitted sitting-room. I looked in, half fearfully, but, although all the lights were turned on, the room was empty. McBride crossed the room quickly, opened a door to a bedroom, and jerked his head back with a quick motion, signifying his desire for us to follow.

Stretched lifeless on the white linen of the immaculate bed lay the form of a woman, a beautiful woman she had been, too, though not with the freshness which makes American women so attractive. There was something artificial about her beauty, the artificiality which hinted at a hidden story of a woman with a past.

She was a foreigner, apparently of one of the Latin races, although at the moment in the horror of the tragedy before us I could not guess her nationality. It was enough for me that here lay this cold, stony, rigid beauty, robed in the latest creations of Paris, alone in an elegantly furnished room of an exclusive hotel where hundreds of gay guests were dining and chatting and laughing without a suspicion of the terrible secret only a few feet distant from them.

We stood awestruck for the moment.

"The coroner ought to be here any moment," remarked McBride and even the callousness of the regular detective was not sufficient to hide the real feelings of the man. His practical sense soon returned, however, and he continued, "Now, Jameson, don't you think you could use a little influence with the newspaper men to keep this thing off the front pages? Of course something has to be printed about it. But we don't want to hoodoo the hotel right at the start. We had a suicide the other day who left an apologetic note that was played up by some of the papers. Now comes this affair. The management are just as anxious to have the crime cleared up as any one - if it is a crime. But can't it be done with the soft pedal? We will stop at nothing in the way of expense - just so long as the name of the Vanderveer is kept in the background. Only, I'm afraid the coroner will try to rub it in and make the thing sensational."

"What was her name?" asked Kennedy. "At least, under what name was she registered?

"She was registered as Madame de Nevers. It is not quite a week now since she came here, came directly from the steamer Tripolitania. See, there are her trunks and things, all pasted over with foreign labels, not an American label among them. I haven't the slightest doubt that her name was fictitious, for as far as I can see all the ordinary marks of identification have been obliterated. It will take time to identify her at the best, and in the meantime, if a crime has been committed, the guilty person may escape. What I want now, right away, is action."

"Has nothing in her actions about the hotel offered any clue, no matter how slight?" asked Kennedy.

"Plenty of things," replied McBride quickly. "For one thing, she didn't speak very much English and her maid seemed to do all the talking for her, even to ordering her meals, which were always served here. I did notice Madame a few times about the hotel, though she spent most of her time in her rooms. She was attractive as the deuce, and the men all looked at her whenever she stirred out. She never even noticed them. But she was evidently expecting some one, for her maid had left word at the desk that if a Mr. Gonzales called, she was at home; if any one else, she was out. For the first day or two she kept herself closely confined, except that at the end of the second day she took a short spin through the park in a taxicab - closed, even in this hot weather. Where she went I cannot say, but when they returned the maid seemed rather agitated. At least she was a few minutes later when she came all the way downstairs to telephone from a booth, instead of using the room telephone. At various times the maid was sent out to execute certain errands, but always returned promptly. Madame de Nevers was a genuine woman of mystery, but as long as she was a quiet mystery, I thought it no business of ours to pry into the affairs of Madame."

"Did she have any visitors? Did this Mr. Gonzales call?" asked Kennedy at length.

"She had one visitor, a woman who called and asked if a Madame de Nevers was stopping at the hotel," answered McBride. "That was what the clerk was telling me when I happened to catch sight of you. He says that, obedient to the orders from the maid, he told the visitor that Madame was not at home."

"Who was this visitor, do you suppose?" asked Craig. "Did she leave any card or message? Is there any clue to her?"

The detective looked at him earnestly for a time as if he hesitated to retail what might be merely pure gossip.

"The clerk does not know this absolutely, but from his acquaintance with society news and the illustrated papers he is sure that he recognised her. He says that he feels positive that it was Miss Catharine Lovelace."

"The Southern heiress," exclaimed Kennedy. "Why, the papers say that she is engaged "

"Exactly," cut in McBride, "the heiress who is rumoured to be engaged to the Duc de Chateaurouge.

Kennedy and I exchanged, glances. "Yes," I added, recollecting a remark I had heard a few days before from our society reporter on the Star, "I believe it has been said that Chateaurouge is in this country, incognito."

"A pretty slender thread on which to hang an identification," McBride hastened to remark. "Newspaper photographs are not the best means of recognising anybody. Whatever there may be in it, the fact remains that Madame de Nevers, supposing that to be her real name, has been dead for at least a day or two. The first thing to be determined is whether this is a death from natural causes, a suicide, or a murder. After we have determined that we shall be in a position to run down this Lovelace clue."

Kennedy said nothing and I could not gather whether he placed greater or less value on the suspicion of the hotel clerk. He had been making a casual examination of the body on the bed, and finding nothing he looked intently about the room as if seeking some evidence of how the crime had been committed.

To me the thing seemed incomprehensible, that without an outcry being overheard by any of the guests a murder could have been done in a crowded hotel in which the rooms on every side had been occupied and people had been passing through the halls at all hours. Had it indeed been a suicide, in spite of McBride's evident conviction to the contrary?

A low exclamation from Kennedy attracted our attention. Caught in the filmy lace folds of the woman's dress he had found a few small and thin pieces of glass. He was regarding them with an interest that was oblivious to everything else. As he turned them over and over and tried to fit them together they seemed to form at least a part of what had once been a hollow globe of very thin glass, perhaps a quarter of an inch or so in diameter.

"How was the body discovered?" asked Craig at length, looking up at McBride quickly.

"Day before yesterday Madame's maid went to the cashier," repeated the detective slowly as if rehearsing the case as much for his own information as ours, "and said that Madame had asked her to say to him that she was going away for a few days and that under no circumstances was her room to be disturbed in her absence. The maid was commissioned to pay the bill, not only for the time they had been here, but also for the remainder of the week, when Madame would most likely return, if not earlier. The bill was made out and paid.

"Since then only the chambermaid has entered this suite. The key to that closet over in the corner was gone, and it might have hidden its secret until the end of the week or perhaps a day or two longer, if the chambermaid hadn't been a bit curious. She hunted till she found another key that fitted, and opened the closet door, apparently to see what Madame had been so particular to lock up in her absence. There lay the body of Madame, fully dressed, wedged into the narrow space and huddled up in a corner. The chambermaid screamed and the secret was out."

"And Madame de Nevers's maid? What has become of her?" asked Kennedy eagerly.

"She has disappeared," replied McBride. "From the moment when the bill was paid no one about the hotel has seen her."

"But you have a pretty good description of her, one that you could send out in order to find her if necessary?"

"Yes, I think I could give a pretty good description."

Kennedy's eye encountered the curious gaze of McBride. "This may prove to be a most unusual case," he remarked in answer to the implied inquiry of the detective. "I suppose you have heard of the 'endormeurs' of Paris?"

McBride shook his head in the negative.

"It is a French word signifying a person who puts another to sleep, the sleep makers," explained Kennedy. "They are the latest scientific school of criminals who use the most potent, quickest-acting stupefying drugs. Some of their exploits surpass anything hitherto even imagined by the European police. The American police have been officially warned of the existence of the endormeurs and full descriptions of their methods and photographs of their paraphernalia have been sent over here.

"There is nothing in their repertoire so crude as chloral or knock-out drops. All the derivatives of opium such as morphine, codeine, heroine, dionine, narceine, and narcotine, to say nothing of bromure d'etyle, bromoform, nitrite d'amyle, and amyline are known to be utilised by the endormeurs to put their victims to sleep, and the skill which they have acquired in the use of these powerful drugs establishes them as one of the most dangerous groups of criminals in existence. The men are all of superior intelligence and daring; the chief requisite of the women is extreme beauty as well as unscrupulousness.

"They will take a little thin glass ball of one of these liquids, for instance, hold it in a pocket handkerchief, crush it, shove it under the nose of their victim, and - whiff ! - the victim is unconscious. But ordinarily the endormeur does not kill. He is usually satisfied to stupefy, rob, and then leave his victim. There is something more to this case than a mere suicide or murder, McBride. Of course she may have committed suicide with the drugs of the endormeurs; then again she may merely have been rendered unconscious by those drugs and some other poison may have been administered. Depend on it, there is something more back of this affair than appears on the surface. Even as far as I have gone I do not hesitate to say that we have run across the work of one or perhaps a band of the most up-to-date and scientific criminals."

Kennedy had scarcely finished when McBride brought his right fist down with a resounding smack into the palm of his left hand.

" Say," he cried in great excitement, "here's another thing which may or may not have some connection with the case. The evening after Madame arrived, I happened to be walking through the cafe, where I saw a face that looked familiar to me. It was that of a dark-haired, olive-skinned man, a fascinating face, but a face to be afraid of. I remembered him, I thought, from my police experience, as a notorious crook who had not been seen in New York for years, a man who in the old days used to gamble with death in South American revolutions, a soldier of fortune.

"Well, I gave the waiter, Charley, the wink and he met me in the rear of the cafe, around a corner. You know we have a regular system in the hotel by which I can turn all the help into amateur sleuths. I told him to be very careful about the dark-faced man and the younger man who was with him, to be particular to wait on them well, and to pick up any scraps of conversation he could.

"Charley knows his business, and the barest perceptible sign from me makes him an obsequious waiter. Of course the dark man didn't notice it at the time, but if he had been more observant he would have seen that three times during his chat with his companion Charley had wiped off his table with lingering hand. Twice he had put fresh seltzer in his drink. Like a good waiter always working for a big tip he had hovered near, his face blank and his eyes unobservant. But that waiter was an important link in my chain of protection of the hotel against crooks. He was there to listen and to tip me off, which he did between orders.

"There wasn't much that he overheard, but what there was of it was so suspicious that I did not hesitate to conclude that the fellow was an undesirable guest. It was something about the Panama Canal, and a coaling station of a steamship and fruit concern on the shore of one of the Latin American countries. It was, he said, in reality to be the coaling station of a certain European power which he did not name but which the younger man seemed to understand. They talked of wharves and tracts of land, of sovereignty and blue prints, the Monroe Doctrine, value in case of war, and a lot of other things. Then they talked of money, and though Charley was most assiduous at the time all he overheard was something about 'ten thousand francs' and 'buying her off,' and finally a whispered confidence of which he caught the words, 'just a blind to get her over here, away from Paris.' Finally the dark man in an apparent burst of confidence said something about 'the other plans being the real thing after all,' and that the whole affair would bring him in fifty thousand francs, with which he could afford to be liberal. Charley could get no inkling about what that other thing was.

"But I felt sure that he had heard enough to warrant the belief that some kind of confidence game was being discussed. To tell the truth I didn't care much what it was, at the time. It might have been an attempt of the dark-visaged fellow to sell the Canal to a come-on. What I wanted was to have it known that the Vanderveer was not to be a resort of such gentry as this. But I'm afraid it was much more serious than I thought at the time.

"Well, the dark man finally excused himself and sauntered into the lobby and up to the desk, with me after him around the opposite way. He was looking over the day's arrivals on the register when I concluded that it was about time to do something. I was standing directly beside him lighting a cigar. I turned quickly on him and deliberately trod on the man's patent leather shoe. He faced me furiously at not getting any apology. 'Sacre,' he exclaimed, 'what the -' But before he could finish I moved still closer and pinched his elbow. A dull red glow of suppressed anger spread over his face, but he cut his words short. He knew and I knew he knew. That is the sign in the continental hotels when they find a crook and quietly ask him to move on. The man turned on his heel and stalked out of the hotel. By and by the young man in the cafe, considerably annoyed at the sudden inattention of the waiter who acted as if he wasn't satisfied with his tip, strolled through the lobby and not seeing his dark-skinned friend, also disappeared. I wish to heaven I had had them shadowed. The young fellow wasn't a come-on at all. There was something afoot between these two, mark my words."

"But why do you connect that incident with this case of Madame de Nevers?" asked Kennedy, a little puzzled.

"Because the next day, and the day that Madame's maid disappeared, I happened to see a man bidding good-bye to a woman at the rear carriage entrance of the hotel. The woman was Madame's maid and the man was the dark man who had been seated in the cafe."

"You said a moment ago that you had a good description of the maid or could write one. Do you think you could locate her?"

The hotel detective thought a minute or two. "If she has gone to any of the other hotels in this city, I could," he answered slowly. "You know we have recently formed a sort of clearing house, we hotel detectives, and we are working together now very well, though secretly. It is barely possible that she has gone to another hotel. The very brazenness of that would be its safeguard, she might think."

"Then I can leave that part of it to you, McBride?" asked Kennedy thoughtfully as if laying out a programme of action in his mind. "You will set the hotel detectives on the trail as well as the police of the city, and of other cities, will make the inquiries at the steamships and railroads, and all that sort of thing? Try to find some trace of the two men whom you saw in the cafe at the same time. But for the present I should say spare no effort to locate that girl."

"Trust it to me," agreed McBride confidently. A heavy tap sounded at the door and McBride opened it. It was the coroner.

I shall not go into the lengthy investigation which the coroner conducted, questioning one servant and employee after another without eliciting any more real information than we had already obtained so concisely from the house man. The coroner was, of course, angry at the removal of the body from the closet to the bed because he wanted to view it in the position in which it had been found, but as that had been done by the servants before McBride could stop them, there was nothing to do about it but accept the facts.

"A very peculiar case," remarked the coroner at the conclusion of his examination, with the air of a man who could shed much light on it from his wide experience if he chose. "There is just one point that we shall have to clear up, however. What was the cause of the death of the deceased? There is no gas in the room. It couldn't have been illuminating gas, then. No, it must have been a poison of some kind. Then as to the motive," he added, trying to look confident but really shooting a tentative remark at Craig and the house detective, who said nothing. "It looks a good deal like that other suicide - at least a suicide which some one has endeavoured to conceal," he added, hastily recollecting the manner in which the body had been found and his criticisms of the removal from the closet.

"Didn't I tell you?" rejoined McBride dolefully after we had left the coroner downstairs a few minutes later. "I knew he would think the hotel was hiding something from him."

"We can't help what he thinks - yet," remarked Craig. "All we can do is to run down the clues which we have. I will leave the maid to be found by your organisation, McBride. Let me see, the theatres and roof gardens must be letting out by this time. I will see if I can get any information from Miss Lovelace. Find her address, Walter, and call a cab."

The Southern heiress, who had attracted more attention by her beauty than by her fortune which was only moderate as American fortunes go nowadays, lived in an apartment facing the park, with her mother, a woman whose social ambitions it was commonly known had no bounds and were often sadly imposed upon.

Fortunately we arrived at the apartment not very many minutes after the mother and daughter, and although it was late, Kennedy sent up his card with an urgent message to see them. They received us in a large drawing-room and were plainly annoyed by our visit, though that of course was susceptible of a natural interpretation.

"What is it that you wished to see me about?" began Mrs. Lovelace in a tone which was intended to close the interview almost before it was begun. Kennedy had not wished to see her about anything, but of course he did not even hint as much in his reply which was made to her but directed at Miss Lovelace.

"Could you tell me anything about a Madame de Nevers who was staying at the Vanderveer?" asked Craig, turning quickly to the daughter so as to catch the full effect of his question, and then waiting as if expecting the answer from her.

The young lady's face blanched slightly and she seemed to catch her breath for an instant, but she kept her composure admirably in spite of the evident shock of Craig's purposely abrupt question.

"I have heard of her," Miss Lovelace replied with forced calmness as he continued to look to her for an answer. "Why do you ask?"

"Because a woman who is supposed to be Madame de Nevers has committed suicide at the Vanderveer and it was thought that perhaps you could identify her."

By this time she had become perfect mistress of herself again, from which I argued that whatever knowledge she had of Madame was limited to the time before the tragedy.

"I, identify her? Why, I never saw her. I simply know that such a creature exists.

She said it defiantly and with an iciness which showed more plainly than in mere words that she scorned even an acquaintance with a demi-mondaine.

"Do you suppose the Duc de Chateaurouge would be able to identify her?" asked Kennedy mercilessly. "One moment, please," he added, anticipating the blank look of amazement on her face. "I have reason to believe that the duke is in this country incognito - is he not?"

Instead of speaking she merely raised her shoulders a fraction of an inch.

"Either in New York or in Washington," pursued Kennedy.

"Why do you ask me?" she said at length. "Isn't it enough that some of the newspapers have said so? If you see it in the newspapers, it's so - perhaps - isn't it?"

We were getting nowhere in this interview, at least so I thought. Kennedy cut it short, especially as he noted the evident restlessness of Mrs. Lovelace. However, he had gained his point. Whether or not the duke was in New York or Washington or Spitzbergen, he now felt sure that Miss Lovelace knew of, and perhaps something about, Madame de Nevers. In some way the dead woman had communicated with her and Miss Lovelace had been the woman whom the hotel clerk had seen at the Vanderveer. We withdrew as gracefully as our awkward position permitted.

As there was nothing else to be done at that late hour, Craig decided to sleep soundly over the case, his infallible method of taking a fresh start after he had run up a cul-de-sac.

Imagine our surprise in the morning at being waited on by the coroner himself, who in a few words explained that he was far from satisfied with the progress his own office was making with the case.

"You understand," he concluded after a lengthy statement of confession and avoidance, "we have no very good laboratory facilities of our own to carry out the necessary chemical, pathological, and bacteriological investigations in cases of homicide and suicide. We are often forced to resort to private laboratories, as you know in the past when I have had to appeal to you. Now, Professor Kennedy, if we might turn over that research part of the case to you, sir, I will engage to see that a reasonable bill for your professional services goes through the office of my friend the city comptroller promptly."

Craig snapped at the opportunity, though he did not allow the coroner to gain that impression.

"Very well," agreed that official, " I shall see that all the necessary organs for a thorough test as to the cause of the death of this woman are sent up to the Chemistry Building right away."

The coroner was as good as his word, and we had scarcely breakfasted and arrived at Craig's scientific workshop before that official appeared, accompanied by a man who carried in uncanny jars the necessary materials for an investigation following an autopsy.

Kennedy was now in his element. The case had taken an unexpected turn which made him a leading factor in its solution. Whatever suspicions he may have entertained unofficially the night before he could now openly and quickly verify.

He took a little piece of lung tissue and with sharp sterilised knife cut it up. Then he made it slightly alkaline with a little sodium carbonate, talking half to us and half to himself as he worked. The next step was to place the matter in a glass flask in a water bath where it was heated. From the flask a Bohemian glass tube led into a cool jar and on a part of the tube a flame was playing which heated it to redness for two or three inches.

Several minutes we waited in silence. Finally when the process had gone far enough, Kennedy took a piece of paper which had been treated with iodised starch, as he later explained. He plunged the paper into the cool jar. Slowly it turned a strong blue tint.

Craig said nothing, but it was evident that he was more than gratified by what had happened. He quickly reached for a bottle on the shelves before him, and I could see from the label on the brown glass that it was nitrate of silver. As he plunged a little in a test-tube into the jar a strong precipitate was gradually formed.

"It is the decided reaction for chloroform," he exclaimed simply in reply to our unspoken questions.

"Chloroform," repeated the coroner, rather doubtfully, and it was evident that he had expected a poison and had not anticipated any result whatever from an examination of the lungs instead of the stomach to which he had confined his own work so far. "Could chloroform be discovered in the lungs or viscera after so many days? There was one famous chloroform case for which a man is now serving a life term in Sing Sing which I have understood there was grave doubt in the minds of the experts. Mind, I am not trying to question the results of your work except as they might naturally be questioned in court. It seems to me that the volatility of chloroform might very possibly preclude its discovery after a short time. Then again, might not other substances be generated in a dead body which would give a reaction very much like chloroform? We must consider all these questions before we abandon the poison theory, sir. Remember, this is the summer time too, and chloroform would evaporate very much more rapidly now than in winter.

Kennedy smiled, but his confidence remained unshaken.

"I am in a position to meet all of your objections," he explained simply. "I think I could lay it down as a rule that by proper methods chloroform may be discovered in the viscera much longer after death than is commonly supposed - in summer from six days to three weeks, with a practical working range of say twelve days, while in winter it may be found even after several months - by the right method. Certainly this case comes within the average length of time. More than that, no substance is generated by the process of decomposition which will vitiate the test for chloroform which I have just made. Chloroform has an affinity for water and is also a preservative, and hence from all these facts I think it safe to conclude that sometimes traces of it may be found for two weeks after its administration, certainly for a few days."

"And Madame de Nevers? "queried the coroner, as if the turn of events was necessitating a complete reconstruction of his theory of the case.

"Was murdered," completed Kennedy in a tone that left nothing more to be said on the subject.

"But," persisted the coroner, "if she was murdered by the use of chloroform, how do you account for the fact that it was done without a struggle? There were no marks of violence and I, for one, do not believe that under ordinary circumstances any one will passively submit to such an administration without a hard fight."

>From his pocket Kennedy drew a small pasteboard box filled with tiny globes, some bonbons and lozenges, a small hypodermic syringe, and a few cigars and cigarettes. He held it out in the palm of his hand so that we could see it.

"This," he remarked, "is the standard equipment of the endormeur. Whoever obtained admittance to Madame's rooms, either as a matter of course or secretly, must have engaged her in conversation, disarmed suspicion, and then suddenly she must have found a pocket handkerchief under her nose. The criminal crushed a globe of liquid in the handkerchief, the victim lost consciousness, the chloroform was administered without a struggle, all marks of identification were obliterated, the body was placed in the closet, and the maid - either as principal or accessory - took the most likely means of postponing discovery by paying the bill in advance at the office, and then disappeared."

Kennedy slipped the box back into his pocket. The coroner had, I think, been expecting Craig's verdict, although he was loath to abandon his own suicide theory and had held it to the last possible moment. At any rate, so far he had said little, apparently preferring to keep his own counsel as to his course of action and to set his own machinery in motion.

He drew a note from his pocket, however. "I suppose," he began tentatively, shaking the note as he glanced doubtfully from it to us, "that you have heard that among the callers on this unfortunate woman was a lady of high social position in this city?"

"I have heard a rumour to that effect," replied Kennedy as he busied himself cleaning up the apparatus he had just used. There was nothing in his manner even to hint at the fact that we had gone further and interviewed the young lady in question.

"Well," resumed the coroner, "in view of what you have just discovered I don't mind telling you that I believe it was more than a rumour. I have had a man watching the woman and this is a report I received just before I came up here."

We read the note which he now handed to us. It was just a hasty line: "Miss Lovelace left hurriedly for Washington this morning."

What was the meaning of it? Clearly, as we probed deeper into the case, its ramifications grew wider than anything we had yet expected. Why had Miss Lovelace gone to Washington, of all places, at this torrid season of the year?

The coroner had scarcely left us, more mystified than ever, when a telephone message came from McBride saying that he had some important news for us if we would meet him at the St. Cenis Hotel within an hour. He would say nothing about it over the wire.

As Kennedy hung up the receiver he quietly took a pistol from a drawer of his desk, broke it quickly, and looked thoughtfully at the cartridges in the cylinder. Then he snapped it shut and stuck it into his pocket.

"There's no telling what we may run up against before we get back to the laboratory," he remarked and we rode down to meet McBride.

The description which the house man had sent out to the other hotel detectives the night before had already produced a result. Within the past two days a man answering the description of the younger man whom McBride had seen in the cafe and a woman who might very possibly have been Madame's maid had come to the St. Cenis as M. and Mme. Duval. Their baggage was light, but they had been at pains to impress upon the hotel that they were persons of some position and that it was going direct from the railroad to the steamer, after their tour of America. They had, as a matter of fact, done nothing to excite suspicion until the general request for information had been received.

The house man of the St. Cenis welcomed us cordially upon McBride's introduction and agreed to take us up to the rooms of the strange couple if they were not in. As it happened it was the lunch hour and they were not in the room. Still, Kennedy dared not be too particular in his search of their effects, for he did not wish to arouse suspicion upon their return, at least not yet.

"It seems to me, Craig," I suggested after we had nosed about for a few minutes, finding nothing, "that this is pre-eminently a case in which to use the dictograph as you did in that Black Hand case."

He shook his head doubtfully, although I could see that the idea appealed to him. "The dictograph has been getting too much publicity lately," he said. "I'm afraid they would discover it, that is, if they are at all the clever people I think them. Besides, I would have to send up to the laboratory to get one and by the time the messenger returned they might be back from lunch. No, we've got to do something else, and do it quickly."

He was looking about the room in an apparently aimless manner. On the side wall hung a cheap etching of a woodland scene. Kennedy seemed engrossed in it while the rest of us fidgeted at the delay.

"Can you get me a couple of old telephone instruments?" he asked at length, turning to us and addressing the St. Cenis detective.

The detective nodded and disappeared down the hall. A few minutes later he deposited the instruments on a table. Where he got them I do not know, but I suspect he simply lifted them from vacant rooms.

"Now some Number 30 copper wire and a couple of dry cells," ordered Kennedy, falling to work immediately on the telephones. The detective despatched a bellboy down to the basement to get the wire from the house electrician.

Kennedy removed the transmitters of the telephones, and taking the carbon capsules from them placed the capsules on the table carefully. Then he lifted down the etching from the wall and laid it flat on its face before us. Quickly he removed the back of the picture.

Pressing the transmitter fronts with the carbon capsules against the paper and the glass on the picture he mounted them so that the paper and glass acted as a large diaphragm to collect all the sounds in the room.

"The size of this glass diaphragm," he explained as we gathered around in intense interest at what he was doing, "will produce a strikingly sensitive microphone action and the merest whisper will be reproduced with startling distinctness."

The boy brought the wire up and also the news that the couple in whose room we were had very nearly finished luncheon and might be expected back in a few minutes.

Kennedy took the tiny wires, and after connecting them hung up the picture again and ran them up alongside the picture wires leading from the huge transmitter up to the picture moulding. Along the top of the moulding and out through the transom it was easy enough to run the wires and so down the hall to a vacant room, where Craig attached them quickly to one of the old telephone receivers.

Then we sat down in this room to await developments from our hastily improvised picture frame microphone detective.

At last we could hear the elevator door close on our floor. A moment later it was evident from the expression of Kennedy's face that some one had entered the room which we had just left. He had finished not a moment too soon.

"It's a good thing that I didn't wait to put a dictograph there," he remarked to us. "I thought I wasn't reckoning without reason. The couple, whoever they are, are talking in undertones and looking about the room to see if anything has been disturbed in their absence."

Kennedy alone, of course, could follow over his end of the telephone what they said. The rest of us could do nothing but wait, but from notes which Craig jotted down as he listened to the conversation I shall reproduce it as if we had all heard it. There were some anxious moments until at last they had satisfied themselves that no one was listening and that no dictograph or other mechanical eavesdropper, such as they had heard of, was concealed in the furniture or back of it.

"Why are you so particular, Henri?" a woman's voice was saying.

"Louise, I've been thinking for a long time that we are surrounded by spies in these hotels. You remember I told you what happened at the Vanderveer the night you and Madame arrived? I'm sure that waiter overheard what Gonzales and I were talking about."

"Well, we are safe now anyhow. What was it that you would not tell me just now at luncheon?" asked the woman, whom Kennedy recognised as Madame de Nevers's maid.

"I have a cipher from Washington. Wait until I translate it."

There was a pause. "What does it say?" asked the woman impatiently.

"It says," repeated the man slowly, "that Miss Lovelace has gone to Washington. She insists on knowing whether the death of Marie was a suicide or not. Worse than that the Secret Service must have wind of some part of our scheme, for they are acting suspiciously. I must go down there or the whole affair may be exposed and fall through. Things could hardly be worse, especially this sudden move on her part."

"Who was that detective who forced his way to see her the night they discovered Marie's body?" asked the woman. "I hope that that wasn't the Secret Service also. Do you think they could have suspected anything?"

"I hardly think so," the man replied. "Beyond the death of Madame they suspect nothing here in New York, I am convinced. You are sure that all her letters were secured, that all clues to connect her with the business in hand were destroyed, and particularly that the package she was to deliver is safe?"

"The package? You mean the plans for the coaling station on the Pacific near the Canal? You see, Henri, I know."

"Ha, ha, - yes," replied the man. "Louise, shall I tell you a secret? Can you keep it?"

"You know I can, Henri."

"Well, Louise, the scheme is deeper than even you think. We are playing one country against another, America against - you know the government our friend Schmidt works for in Paris. Now, listen. Those plans of the coaling station are a fake - a fake. It is just a commercial venture. No nation would be foolish enough to attempt such a thing, yet. We know that they are a fake. But we are going to sell them through that friend of ours in the United States War Department. But that is only part of the coup, the part that will give us the money to turn the much larger coups we have in the future. You can understand why it has all to be done so secretly and how vexatious it is that as soon as one obstacle is overcome a dozen new ones appear. Louise, here is the big secret. By using those fake plans as a bait we are going to obtain something which when we all return to Paris we can convert into thousands of francs. There, I can say no more. But I have told you so much to impress upon you the extreme need of caution."

"And how much does Miss Lovelace know?"

"Very little - I hope. That is why I must go to Washington myself. She must know nothing of this coup nor of the real de Nevers, or the whole scheme may fall through. It would have fallen through before, Louise, if you had failed us and had let any of de Nevers's letters slip through to Miss Lovelace. She richly deserved her fate for that act of treachery. The affair would have been so simple, otherwise. Luck was with us until her insane jealousy led her to visit Miss Lovelace. It was fortunate the young lady was out when Madame called on her or all would have been lost. Ah, we owe you a great deal, Louise, and we shall not forget it, never. You will be very careful while I am gone?"

"Absolutely. When will you return to me, Henri?"

"To-morrow morning at the latest. This afternoon the false coaling station plans are to be turned over to our accomplice in the War Department and in exchange he is to give us something else - the secret of which I spoke. You see the trail leads up into high circles. It is very much more important than you suppose and discovery might lead to a dangerous international complication just now."

"Then you are to meet your friend in Washington to-night? When do you start, Henri? Don't let the time slip by. There must be no mistake this time as there was when we were working for Japan and almost had the blue prints of Corregidor at Manila only to lose them on the streets of Calcutta."

"Trust me. We are to meet about nine o'clock and therefore I leave on the limited at three-thirty, in about an hour. From the station I am going straight to the house on Z Street - let me see, the cipher says the number is 101 - and ask for a man named Gonzales. I shall use the name Montez. He is to appear, hand over the package - that thing I have told you about - then I am to return here by one of the midnight trains. At any cost we must allow nothing to happen which will reach the ears of Miss Lovelace. I'll see you early to-morrow morning, ma cherie, and remember, be ready, for the Aquitania sails at ten. The division of the money is to be made in Paris. Then we shall all go our separate ways."

Kennedy was telephoning frantically through the regular hotel service to find out how the trains ran for Washington. The only one that would get there before nine was the three-thirty; the next, leaving an hour later, did not arrive until nearly eleven. He had evidently had some idea of causing some delay that would result in our friend down the hall missing the limited, but abandoned it. Any such scheme would simply result in a message to the gang in Washington putting them on their guard and defeating his purpose.

"At all costs we must beat this fellow to it," exclaimed Craig, waiting to hear no more over his improvised dictograph. "Come, Walter, we must catch the limited for Washington immediately. McBride, I leave you and the regular house man to shadow this woman. Don't let her get out of your sight for a moment."

As we rode across the city to the new railroad terminus Craig hastily informed me of what he had overheard. We took up our post so that we could see the outgoing travellers, and a few minutes later Craig spotted our man from McBride's description, and succeeded in securing chairs in the same car in which he was to ride.

Taken altogether it was an uneventful journey. For five mortal hours we sat in the Pullman or toyed with food in the dining-car, never letting the man escape our sight, yet never letting him know that we were watching him. Nevertheless I could not help asking myself what good it did. Why did not Kennedy hire a special if the affair was so important as it appeared? How were we to get ahead of him in Washington better than in New York? I knew that some plan lurked behind the calm and inscrutable face of Kennedy as I tried to read and could not.

The train had come to a stop in the Union Station. Our man was walking rapidly up the platform in the direction of the cab stand. Suddenly Kennedy darted ahead and for a moment we were walking abreast of him.

"I beg your pardon," began Craig as we came to a turn in the shadow of the arc lights, "but have you a match?"

The man halted and fumbled for his match-box. Instantly Kennedy's pocket handkerchief was at his nose.

"Some of the medicine of your own gang of endormeurs," ground out Kennedy, crushing several of the little glass globes under his handkerchief to make doubly sure of their effect.

The man reeled and would have fallen if we had not caught him between us. Up the platform we led him in a daze.

"Here," shouted Craig to a cabman, "my friend is ill. Drive us around a bit. It will sober him up. Come on, Walter, jump in, the air will do us all good."

Those who were in Washington during that summer will remember the suppressed activity in the State, War, and

Navy Departments on a certain very humid night. Nothing leaked out at the time as to the cause, but it was understood later that a crisis was narrowly averted at a very inopportune season, for the heads of the departments were all away, the President was at his summer home in the North, and even some of the under-secretaries were out of town. Hasty messages had been sizzling over the wires in cipher and code for hours.

I recall that as we rode a little out of our way past the Army Building, merely to see if there was any excitement, we found it a blaze of lights. Something was plainly afoot even at this usually dull period of the year. There was treachery of some kind and some trusted employee was involved, I felt instinctively. As for Craig he merely glanced at the insensible figure between us and remarked sententiously that to his knowledge there was only one nation that made a practice of carrying out its diplomatic and other coups in the hot weather, a remark which I understood to mean that our mission was more than commonly important.

The man had not recovered when we arrived within several blocks of our destination, nor did he show signs of recovery from his profound stupor. Kennedy stopped the cab in a side street, pressed a bill into the cabman's hand, and bade him wait until we returned.

We had turned the corner of Z Street and were approaching the house when a man walking in the opposite direction eyed us suspiciously, turned, and followed us a step or two.

"Kennedy!" he exclaimed.

If a fourteen-inch gun had exploded behind us I could not have been more startled. Here, in spite of all our haste and secrecy we were followed, watched, and beaten.

Craig wheeled about suddenly. Then he took the man by the arm. "Come," he said quickly, and we three dove into the shadow of an alley.

As we paused, Kennedy was the first to speak. "By Jove, Walter, it's Burke of the Secret Service," he exclaimed.

"Good," repeated the man with some satisfaction. "I see that you still have that memory for faces." He was evidently referring to our experiences together some months before with the portrait parle and identification in the counterfeiting case which Craig cleared up for him.

For a moment or two Burke and Kennedy spoke in whispers. Under the dim light from the street I could see Kennedy's face intent and working with excitement.

"No wonder the War Department is a blaze of lights," he exclaimed as we moved out of the shadow again, leaving the Secret Service man. "Burke, I had no idea when I took up this case that I should be doing my country a service also. We must succeed at any hazard. The moment you hear a pistol shot, Burke, we shall need you. Force the door if it is not already open. You were right as to the street but not the number. It is that house over there. Come on, Walter."

We mounted the low steps of the house and a negress answered the bell. "Is Mr. Gonzales in?" asked Kennedy.

The hallway into which we were admitted was dark but it opened into a sitting-room, where a dim light was burning behind the thick portieres. Without a word the negress ushered us into this room, which was otherwise empty.

"Tell him Mr. Montez is here," added Craig as we sat down.

The negress disappeared upstairs, and in a few minutes returned with the message that he would be down directly.

No sooner had the shuffle of her footsteps died away than Kennedy was on his feet, listening intently at the door. There was no sound. He took a chair and tiptoed out into the dark hall with it. Turning it upside down he placed it at the foot of the stairs with the four legs pointing obliquely up. Then he drew me into a corner with him.

How long we waited I cannot say. The next I knew was a muffled step on the landing above, then the tread on the stairs.

A crash and a deep volley of oaths in French followed as the man pitched headlong over the chair on the dark steps.

Kennedy whipped out his revolver and fired point-blank at the prostrate figure. I do not know what the ethics are of firing on a man when he is down, nor did I have time to stop to think.

Craig grasped my arm and pulled me toward the door. A sickening odour seemed to pervade the air. Upstairs there was shouting and banging of doors.

"Closer, Walter," he muttered, "closer to the door, and open it a little, or we shall both be suffocated. It was the Secret Service gun I shot off - the pistol that shoots stupefying gas from its vapour-filled cartridges and enables you to put a criminal out of commission without killing him. A pull of the trigger, the cap explodes, the gunpowder and the force of the explosion unite some capsicum and lycopodium, producing the blinding, suffocating vapour whose terrible effect you see. Here, you upstairs," he shouted, "advance an inch or so much as show your heads over the rail and I pump a shot at you, too. Walter, take the gun yourself. Fire at a move from them. I think the gases have cleared away enough now. I must get him before he recovers consciousness."

A tap at the door came, and without taking my eyes off the stairs I opened it. Burke slid in and gulped at the nauseous atmosphere.

"What's up?" he gasped. "I heard a shot. Where's Kennedy?"

I motioned in the darkness. Kennedy's electric bull's-eye flashed up at that instant and we saw him deftly slip a bright pair of manacles on the wrists of the man on the floor, who was breathing heavily, while blood flowed from a few slight cuts due to his fall.

Dexterously as a pickpocket Craig reached into the man's coat, pulled out a packet of papers, and gazed eagerly at one after another. From among them he unfolded one written in French to Madame Marie de Nevers some weeks before. I translate:

DEAR MARIE: Herr Schmidt informs me that his agent in the War Department at Washington, U.S.A., has secured some important information which will interest the Government for which Herr Schmidt is the agent - of course you know who that is.

It is necessary that you should carry the packet which will be handed to you (if you agree to my proposal) to New York by the steamer Tripolitania. Go to the Vandeveer Hotel and in a few days, as soon as a certain exchange can be made, either our friend in Washington or myself will call on you, using the name Gonzales. In return for the package which you carry he will hand you another. Lose no time in bringing the second package back to Paris.

I have arranged that you will receive ten thousand francs and your expenses for your services in this matter. Under no conditions betray your connection with Herr Schmidt. I was to have carried the packet to America myself and make the exchange but knowing your need of money I have secured the work for you. You had better take your maid, as it is much better to travel with distinction in this case. If, however, you accept this commission I shall consider you in honour bound to surrender your claim upon my name for which I agree to pay you fifty thousand francs upon my marriage with the American heiress of whom you know. Please let me know immediately through our mutual friend Henri Duval whether this proposal is satisfactory. Henri will tell you that fifty thousand is my ultimatum.

"The scoundrel," ground out Kennedy. "He lured his wife from Paris to New York, thinking the Paris police too acute for him, I suppose. Then by means of the treachery of the maid Louise and his friend Duval, a crook who would even descend to play the part of valet for him and fall in love with the maid, he has succeeded in removing the woman who stood between him and an American fortune."

"Marie," rambled Chateaurouge as he came blinking, sneezing, and choking out of his stupor, "Marie, you are clever, but not too clever for me. This blackmailing must stop. Miss Lovelace knows something, thanks to you, but she shall never know all - never - never. You - you - ugh! - Stop. Do you think you can hold me back now with those little white hands on my wrists? I wrench them loose - so - and - ugh! - What's this? Where am I?"

The man gazed dazedly at the manacles that held his wrists instead of the delicate hands he had been dreaming of as he lived over the terrible scene of his struggle with the woman who was his wife in the Vanderveer.

"Chateaurouge," almost hissed Kennedy in his righteous wrath, "fake nobleman, real swindler of five continents. Marie de Nevers alive stood in the way of your marriage to the heiress Miss Lovelace. Dead, she prevents it absolutely."

Craig continued to turn over the papers in his hand, as he spoke. At last he came to a smaller packet in oiled silk. As he broke the seal he glanced at it in surprise, then hurriedly exclaimed, "There, Burke. Take these to the War Department and tell them they can turn out their lights and stop their telegrams. This seems to be a copy of our government's plans for the fortification of the Panama Canal, heights of guns, location of searchlights, fire control stations, everything from painstaking search of official and confidential records. That is what this fellow obtained in exchange for his false blue prints of the supposed coaling station on the Pacific.

"I leave the Secret Service to find the leak in the War Department. What I am interested in is not the man who played spy for two nations and betrayed one of them. To me this adventurer who calls himself Chateaurouge is merely the murderer of Madame de Nevers."